GW00730581

For Jariah, Caroline, Lindsey, Ben, Bastion, Stella, Sage, Tre' III & Ned Jr.
Always look for the beauty. Always find the wonder. Always be an authentic witness.

For Lunella
Thank you for your love. Thank you for nourishing me & helping me find my way. I love you.

City of Publication: Jacksonville, Florida

Library of Congress Control Number: 2022918493
ISBN: 979-8-9865096-0-0 (hardback)
ISBN: 979-8-9865096-1-7 (paperback)
ISBN: 979-8-9865096-2-4 (ebook)

The art for this book was created digitally.

Written by
Kristin Murray

Illustrated by
Katura Gaines

NIA'S VIBRANT COLORS

AN AFRICAN AMERICAN MYTHOLOGICAL TALE

Once upon a time,
in a land high above the
heavens, there lived a girl
named Nia. However, Nia
wasn't an ordinary girl.

Nia was an African goddess. Though, she was still trying to figure out what that meant.

Everyone around Nia seemed to have it all figured out. Her mother, Issa, was the goddess of the Earth. Everything that grew from the Earth came from Issa's imagination.

The bright colors of the flowers and each blade of grass was magically connected to her. Even the textured trunks of trees were formed by Issa's flowing locs.

Nia's dad, Zion, was the god of the heavens. He turned night into day and gently put each star in its proper place.

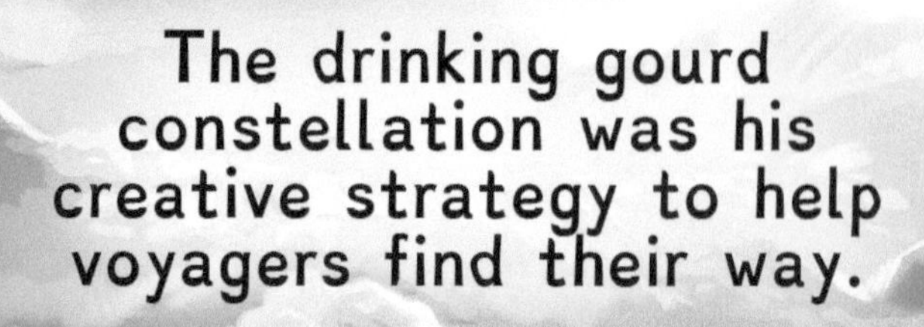

The drinking gourd constellation was his creative strategy to help voyagers find their way.

Everyone seemed to know their way, except Nia.

"Dad?" Nia asked. "How did you know you were supposed to look after the sky?"

"Some things you don't know. Some things you just have to trust," Zion replied.

Nia stared at her dad, confused. Zion pointed at the stars and continued, "Each star in the sky doesn't worry about its purpose. It trusts in its existence. The same elements that make up the stars, make you and me. You're made of stardust." Zion smiled, "Trust your existence and you will shine as bright as the stars."

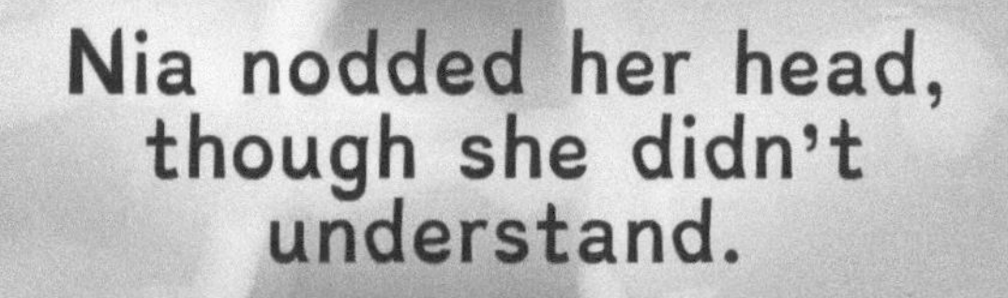

Nia nodded her head, though she didn't understand.

I'M MADE OF STARS?!

She watched quietly as her dad waived his hand and the night sky turned to day.

Unsure of his advice, Nia thought perhaps her mom could help. She hugged her dad and jogged across the sky.

Nia found her mother on the other side of a distant cloud. "Mom," Nia started.

"Yes, sweet girl," her mother replied.

"How did you decide to take care of Earth?"

Issa looked at her inquisitive daughter, impressed by her question.

"I've always believed in being rooted in a purpose," Issa replied. "Reflecting Earth's beauty seemed like a good one."

ROOTED IN PURPOSE?
Nia thought about her mother's words and felt overwhelmed. What did it mean to be rooted in a purpose that brings beauty?
Issa sensed her daughter's confusion. She whispered to Nia, "Simply exist. You'll figure out the rest."
Nia shook her head. Her parents both had the same answers. Yet, none of it made sense to her. "Thanks mom," Nia replied. "I'm going to go paint for a while."

Back in her room, Nia painted with vibrant yellows, oranges and pinks. She loved how these colors made her feel. With each stroke of her paintbrush, Nia started to relax.

Nia was almost done with her painting, when her dad waived his hand toward the sky.
In the blink of an eye, day turned to night.
Nia thought to herself, “I wish there was some sort of warning before that happened.”

She quietly tried to put her paintbrushes back into the jar. Crash! All of the paints and brushes spilled onto Nia's masterpiece. It was too dark for her to see anything or clean up.

"Guess it'll have to wait until morning," she thought.

Frustrated, Nia sat on the edge of her bed and peeped over the clouds to look at the earth below.

This was the first time Nia ever saw the world at night.

There were so many lights! They were bright like the colors in her painting. Nia crawled to get a closer look.

A little closer... a little closer... just a tiny bit more.

Almost there!

There! Now I can see everything!

Uh-oh.

Nia tried to climb back up the clouds, but she couldn't see anything in the dark of night. In that moment she resolved to stay on earth until morning.

Lunella's
Bake Shoppe
She turned around and faced the city's lights. Luckily, there was a bright building across the street. Nia cautiously crossed and walked in.
"Welcome to Lunella's Bakeshop," an older woman greeted. "Are you lost?"
"Kind of," Nia replied.
OPEN

Lunella spoke warmly, “Well come over here and sit for a while. Maybe you’ll remember where you’re going.”
Lunella
Before Nia could make it to the counter, Lunella placed a plate of jellied pastries in front of her. Nia bit into pastry after pastry - blueberry, guava berry, lemon and orange.
Each one was as delicious as the one before it.

Nia noticed the jam jars sitting in front of her.

She reached for extra pink jam and knocked the jars over on the counter. "I'm sorry. That's the second time today I knocked something over."

"Don't worry about it," Lunella replied as the jams ran together.

"In fact," Lunella continued as she dipped her finger in the mixed berry jam, "You just made a beautiful accident. This is delicious!"

Nia tasted the new flavor. "Yum!" she squealed. Nia savored its taste. "What's this pink one?"

"Oh that's my favorite," Lunella replied. "It's called guava berry. Sometimes mistakes make life's most beautiful accidents." The two giggled.

Nia looked at the overlapping flavored jams on the plate. All of the colors and textures looked like a masterpiece. It reminded Nia of her painting back home.
In that moment Nia thought about the advice all the adults gave her:
MORE
CAKE
1. You're made of stardust
2. Be rooted in purpose
3. Beautiful accidents
Just then, the sky switched from night to day.

"I really wish there was a way we could know when night and day were going to switch," Lunella mumbled.
"What if we could?" Nia asked with a smile.
That's when Nia told Lunella where she was from and the big plan she had to help.
"BRILLIANT!!" exclaimed Lunella.
"How will you get back home before it's night time again?" Lunella asked.

Nia smiled.

I AM STARDUST!

She continued, “Thanks for everything Lunella. Make sure you look for the hot pink guava berries.”

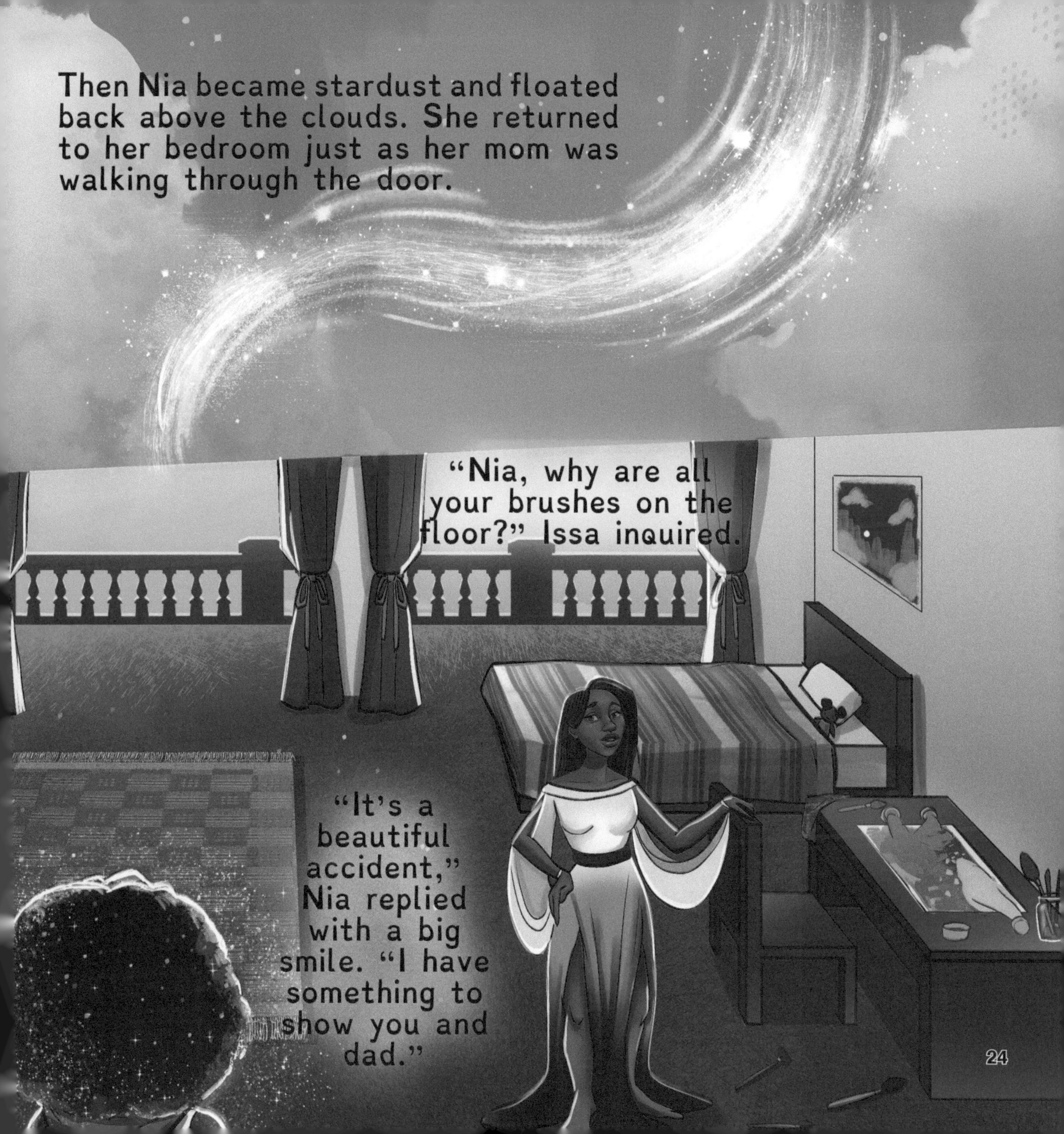

Then Nia became stardust and floated back above the clouds. She returned to her bedroom just as her mom was walking through the door.

“Nia, why are all your brushes on the floor?” Issa inquired.

“It’s a beautiful accident,” Nia replied with a big smile. “I have something to show you and dad.”

Nia explained her incredible adventure to her parents. She told them all about Lunella, mixed berry jam, and how people wanted a warning before day turned to night. Then she held up her painting. "What if I could paint the sky like this to let people know it was almost night time?"

"That's brilliant!"
Nia's dad exclaimed.
Her mom agreed,

Nia used her paintbrushes to cover the sky in vibrant colors. For the first time that day, there were oranges, yellows, purples, and blues just like the plate of mixed berry jam. Then Nia pulled out her paintbrush and added splashes of bright pink. "Thanks for the guava berries," Nia whispered.

Her parents smiled. Their daughter found her purpose by bringing beauty and being herself.

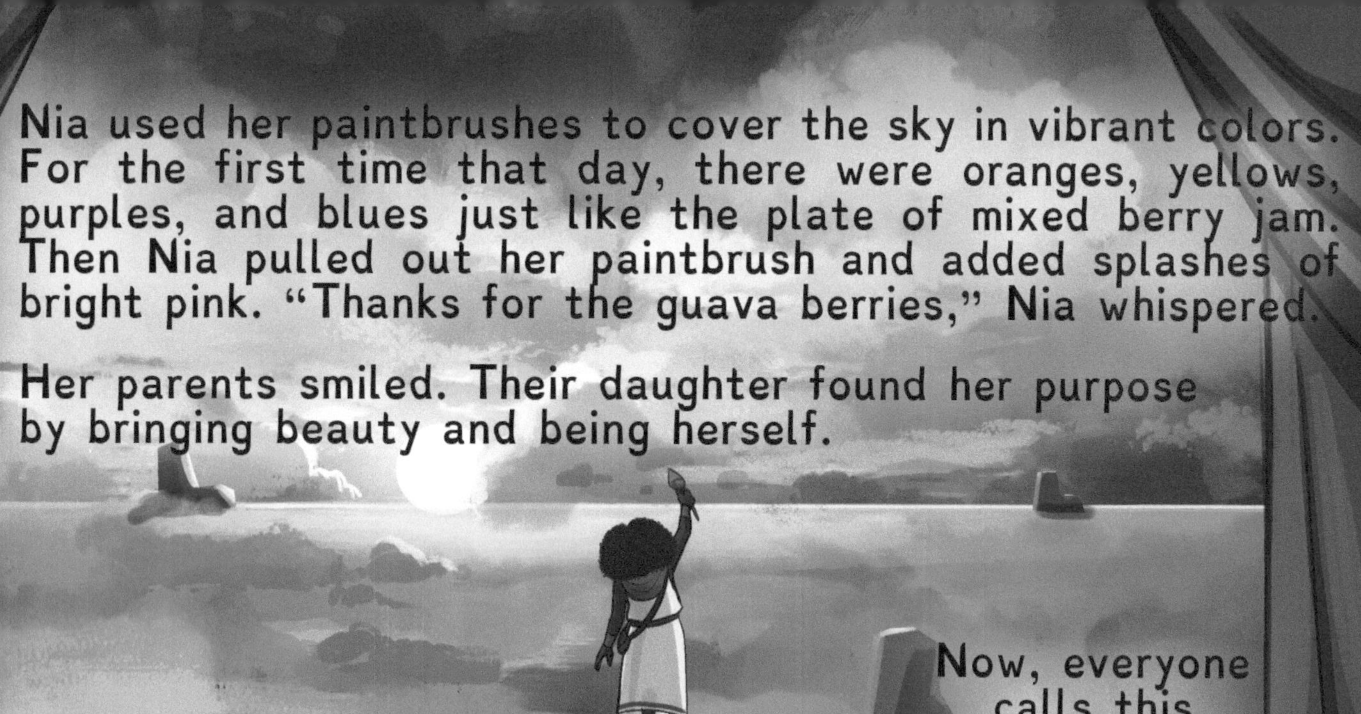

Now, everyone calls this painting sunset. However, for Nia and Lunella, it's a reminder of guava berries, enduring friendship and what can happen when you trust beautiful accidents as you exist.

ABOUT THE AUTHOR

Kristin Murray has loved writing ever since she could pick up a crayon at age two, which led her to earn a Bachelor's Degree in Journalism at Florida A&M University. She's a lover of bright colors, justice and young people finding their voice on this planet. As a life-long children's book collector, she was inspired to write, when she saw a lack of stories about children of color that explored fantasy and mythology. She hopes this book inspires children to keep their spirit of adventure while also staying true to their inner voice.

ABOUT THE ILLUSTRATOR

Katura Gaines is a self-taught digital and traditional artist. At the start of her life, she began drawing anime and cartoons. As she got older, she noticed there weren't a lot of characters who represented the people in her life. To fix this, she began drawing a more diverse array of characters who represented the people around her. Katura's art journey has involved various mediums and styles, and she's worked with several authors to bring their stories and characters to life. She is best known for her personal paintings of vibrant scenes, featuring women of color and soothing palettes.

Lightning Source UK Ltd.
Milton Keynes UK
UKHW052047041122
411546UK00002B/23